THE TOOTH
and
MY FATHER

DOUBLEDAY & COMPANY, INC.
GARDEN CITY, NEW YORK

THE TOOTH
AND
MY FATHER

WILLIAM SAROYAN

Illustrated by Suzanne Verrier

ISBN: 0-385-01697-2 Trade
          0-385-08050-6 Prebound
Library of Congress Catalog Card Number 73–8988
Copyright © 1974 by William Saroyan
All Rights Reserved
Printed in the United States of America
First Edition

THE TOOTH
and
MY FATHER

THE TOOTH

I don't suppose anybody is willing to believe a tooth could come out of a boy's mouth and become another boy and go on and live a life of its own, but what do we care about people who don't believe?

Wouldn't they be surprised if they found out I don't believe in telephone poles, for instance. They're *not* telephone poles. They're trees. They're highly cultivated trees. That's why they're naked, except at the neck, where they put on bow ties. They believe in telephone poles, and I don't. I believe in teeth, and they don't.

I had a tooth one time leaned right over another tooth, like they were old pals, and nobody said, "Go get those teeth straightened." These were the teeth that are right up front at the top, straight down from the nose. The one that leaned over the other was the one on the right—leaning over the one on the left. A lot of people have teeth like that, but more people don't.

Most people have straight regular common-sense teeth, like rabbits, who have the best upper front teeth in the whole world—white, clean, big, and very happy. Do rabbits brush their teeth? No. They don't watch TV, so they don't know that teeth are supposed to be brushed. They just have good straight teeth, not like the leaning tooth that time I'm thinking about. Now, that *was* a tooth, and what happened to it is a story, if I can figure out how to tell it.

I was eight going on nine when I remembered that before the tooth on the right that was leaning on the tooth on the left, there had been another tooth in the same place just like it, which had come out, which I had put under my pillow because during the night the Fairy would come and take the tooth and leave a dime.

Who said so? Everybody said so, but especially my mother. I was very little. How should I know about a thing like that, I thought it was true, I didn't think it was just a nice way to get little kids not to feel bad about the teeth they lose. The baby teeth, I believe they're called. (Another insult. What baby? Who?) Anyhow, the tooth got loose, and the next day it got looser, and there was a lot a family talk about rigging up a front-tooth mechanical device to remove the tooth suddenly and painlessly.

My big sister Zabe invented this device, or at any rate I thought she did. The way it worked was to tie a good long piece of strong thread to the tooth and then to the knob of an open door. Somebody is told to please shut the door. What does he know? He goes and shuts the door real quick. Well, it's either the doorknob or the tooth, so of course it's the tooth.

Only I wouldn't let anybody jolt my leaning tooth out of my leaning head in my leaning body. I didn't believe in that invention, although I knew it worked. It was some kind of super-practical invention that worked perfectly but insulted my feelings, but especially the feelings in my tooth.

Me and my teeth have always been very sensitive about getting insulted. We don't like it. Our point of view is that it isn't courteous. And we both offer and expect courtesy.

And so of course the loose tooth just stayed loose until the next day, and then it became so loose, I almost felt sorry for it, as if something that had once been strong had become weak and was now at death's door.

Why? That was the question. Why was my leaning tooth almost dead in my mouth, getting in the way of speech. Why *my* tooth? Up front that way, and leaning? Was that right? Was it justice? You can bet your life it wasn't. Made me mad. Made me philosophical. Made me stop and think.

What is a boy? What is the sun? Why do cops look like criminals? Why aren't poor people millionaires? And then

all of a sudden I got so tired of the poor dangling tooth and the questions, I took the tooth between my thumb and my forefinger, just to see if maybe I could put it back, make it get strong there again, and be happy again, and not make me ask hard questions. The tooth was very loose, but I was sure it would be glad to be put back in its proper place, so I lifted it up very gently so I wouldn't hurt it and I tried to fit it back, and after a little gentle pushing I thought I had it just right. But when I took my hand away, what do you think happened? I'll tell you what happened. The tooth fell down, dead. Stone dead, cold, free, loose, finished. Was I surprised? The door invention was just another lie. The tooth fell out by itself, and I picked it up.

all of a sudden I got so tired of the poor dangling tooth and the questions, I took the tooth between my thumb and my forefinger, just to see if maybe I could put it back, make it get strong there again, and be happy again, and not make me ask hard questions. The tooth was very loose, but I was sure it would be glad to be put back in its proper place, so I lifted it up very gently so I wouldn't hurt it and I tried to fit it back, and after a little gentle pushing I thought I had it just right. But when I took my hand away, what do you think happened? I'll tell you what happened. The tooth fell down, dead. Stone dead, cold, free, loose, finished. Was I surprised? The door invention was just another lie. The tooth fell out by itself, and I picked it up.

And that night I put it under my pillow, and I thought, "That's the end, that's the end of my good leaning tooth. I'll never see it again. Instead, in the morning I'll see a dime under my pillow."

Well, when I woke up in the morning the tooth was gone. In its place was a nickel and four pennies. This looked to me

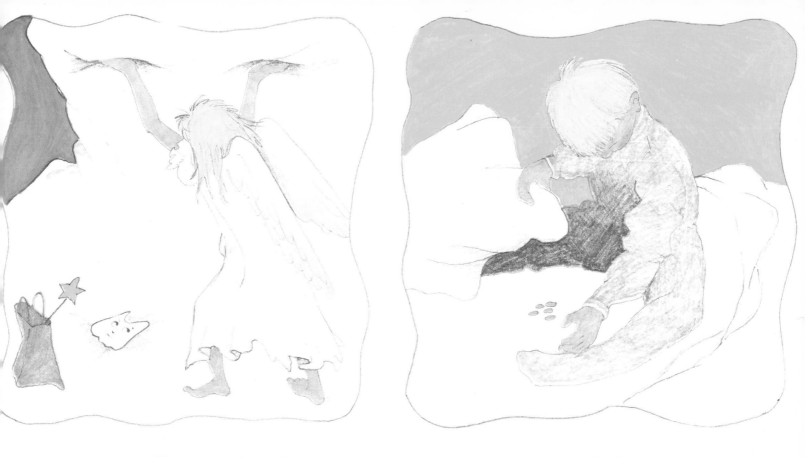

like some kind of a gyp, but I wasn't absolutely sure. I asked everybody in the family if by any chance they had seen my tooth, and they said they hadn't. Well, had they seen the Fairy? Again they said they hadn't, so I showed them the nickel and the four pennies, and I said, "How come the Fairy didn't leave a dime?"

Everybody told me the Fairy runs out of money now and then, too, just like anybody else. I ought to be thankful the Fairy left a nickel and four pennies.

Which is only a little less than a dime, but many more coins than only one little thin dime.

I thought about this: "There's something mysterious going on. I wonder what it is."

Then, years later, when I was eight going on nine and selling papers about the War, I suddenly remembered the lost tooth and I wondered what had become of it—and then like a holy revelation it came to me. That night long ago when I went to sleep the tooth became my real self, and the other self became a nickel and four pennies. It was as simple as that. You gain your soul when you lose your tooth.

This is true. I believe it, and anybody who doesn't believe it—well, maybe he hasn't *got* any teeth.

MY FATHER

My friend, I want to tell you about my father.

My little sister doesn't talk very much and she doesn't know very many words. She crawls a lot but she stands, too. And she can take three or four steps when she tries real hard.

One day she was trying and my father stood in front of her and held out his arms and my little sister walked *fourteen* steps right into his arms.

My little sister was very proud, and my father put her down and she crawled away making all kinds of noises. When she turned around to come back she saw that my father was sitting at a table working with some papers and a pen. My little sister watched him and then she crawled to me and looked at me. I know when she wants to say something, so I waited, and she knew I was waiting, and she kept trying to find the words she wanted. Then at last she said, "Who dat?"

Well, in proper English that would be, "Who is that man?" But I didn't want to hurt my little sister's feelings, so I said, "Dat's my fader." And of course that means, "That's my father."

My little sister said, "Oh." And then she began to crawl in circles, something like some kind of a little animal that is very happy, and she kept saying, "Dat's my fader, dat's my fader."

Well, if he's my father, and she's my little sister, he's her father, too, so that just goes to show you how quickly little kids understand things. But the thing about my father that I want to say is that he is a very good singer. He sings Polly Wolly Doodle, and I guess you know that's the greatest song there is. Some people sing a lot of different words to the music of that song, but my father sings it right, he just sings, "Polly wolly doodle." And he doesn't sing the music the way the other people sing the music, he sings it more like talk.

Our Nurse, Mabel, said to my father one day, "You're not singing it right, you've got the music wrong, and there are other words to the song, there is a whole story, as a matter of fact."

"Oh?" my father said. He sounded just like my little sister, and the expression on his face looked like the expression on her face when she doesn't like what's going on. I thought he was going to cry, maybe, but he just stood there, thinking, thinking real hard, and then he said to our Nurse, "You're fired."

"Well," our Nurse said. "Look who's talking. Look who's being the Boss. Look who's hiring and firing."

We all looked, and there was my father, standing in front of us, looking as if he didn't have a friend in the world, and as if he had just tried very hard to fly and had fallen flat on his face. My little sister turned and looked at me, and she looked just like my father, all hurt, and then she looked at our Nurse, as big as a percheron, and then my little sister crawled to me, so she could be a little back of me, away from our Nurse, Mabel, because this looked like war.

"Who dat?" my little sister said.

"Dat's my fader," I said, but my little sister, she didn't mean him, she meant our Nurse, but I didn't understand right away because I was thinking about my father, and this looked very serious. If Mabel looked like a percheron, my father looked like a pony. Well, did you ever see a pony fight a per-cheron? They just don't do that.

"Who dat?" my little sister said again.

"Dat's Mabel," I said.

"What is Mabel," my little sister said.

"Some kind of great big horse," I whispered. But I guess Mabel heard me because she turned and looked at me, and inasmuch as my little sister was trying to hide behind me she looked at her, too. Then she looked at my father and she said very sweetly, making a cute face, which always scares me to death, because who wants to see somebody like that making a cute face? It has got to mean disaster—tornado, hurricane, shipwreck at sea, explosion, airplane crash, train derailment, and three small, naked birds falling out of a little nest to the sidewalk. Well, *did* they fall, or were they *kicked* out of the nest by a cuckoo, or some other big outlaw bird? Has a cuckoo any right to look cute when it's kicking little birds out of their own private home? I doubt it, but there she stood, our Nurse, Mabel, and she kept looking cute, as she looked from my little sister to me, and on to my little father.

"What did you *say?*" she said. "What did you say, shorty?"

And I prayed that my little father would tell her, tell her again, and I think that if my little sister could think that she would have prayed that my little father would tell her again, too. Sure enough we both heard him with our own ears: "I said you're fired."

"Is that so?" our Nurse said. "Well, let me tell you something, Mr. Bigmouth. I was hired by the Estate when the mother of these two children died, and only the Estate can fire me."

"I *am* the Estate," my father said. "Pack up and go."

"Oh, don't act big, please," our Nurse said to my father. "What would happen to these poor little innocent orphans if I was to leave?"

I AM
THE
ESTATE

"What would happen?" I thought. "What would happen?" my little sister thought. "Why, we'd be happier than we've ever before been, that's what would happen," we both thought. And we both prayed that my father wouldn't give the matter a second thought and hire her back. But we didn't say anything or even move, not even an inch.

We just stayed frozen, waiting for my father to speak. He turned and looked at us and he must have understood how we felt, how we were praying, because he said in a very clear voice, *"I* will take care of my children, so please discontinue the discourtesy and get out of here."

I loved his choice of words, and I watched the cute expression on the face of our Nurse change from superciliousness to astonishment, then disbelief, then anger, and finally rage. She shouted like a Northlady in an opera by Wagner, "Oh. Oh. Oh." She went down the hall, shouting, "Oh. Oh. Oh." She packed a suitcase, shouting, "Oh. Oh. Oh." She walked down the hall and slammed the front door, and we heard her still shouting as she took the shortcut across our lawn to the bus stop on the corner. When she got on the bus, she was still shouting, "Oh. Oh. Oh."

My little sister and I, we hadn't moved, we were afraid if we moved she might say we needed her, and she might come back, so we just watched my father standing at the window, watching our Nurse, and waiting, and my little sister whispered, "Joseph? Who dat?"

"Alice," I said, "dat's my fader."

"My fader, too," Alice said.

"Yes, of course," I said.

My father turned around when the bus disappeared down our street. He wasn't smiling or anything, but we knew he felt

pretty good. He got down on his hands and knees like a real friend, like a real pony, too, and he came up to us very slowly and he said, "Joseph, put your little sister Alice on my back, and then get on behind her, and I'll take you for a little ride around the house."

"No, around the world," I said.

"Yes, I *meant* to say around the world. Ready? Both of you?"

"Yes," we both said, and away we all went, on our way around the world, down the hall, into the kitchen, across the hall into the parlor, through the door, into the nursery, everything in order. As we went by my father knocked over a stack of books, and then he brushed all of our toys off a shelf, and then he pushed over Alice's crib, and then he moved my bed from the corner to the middle of the room.

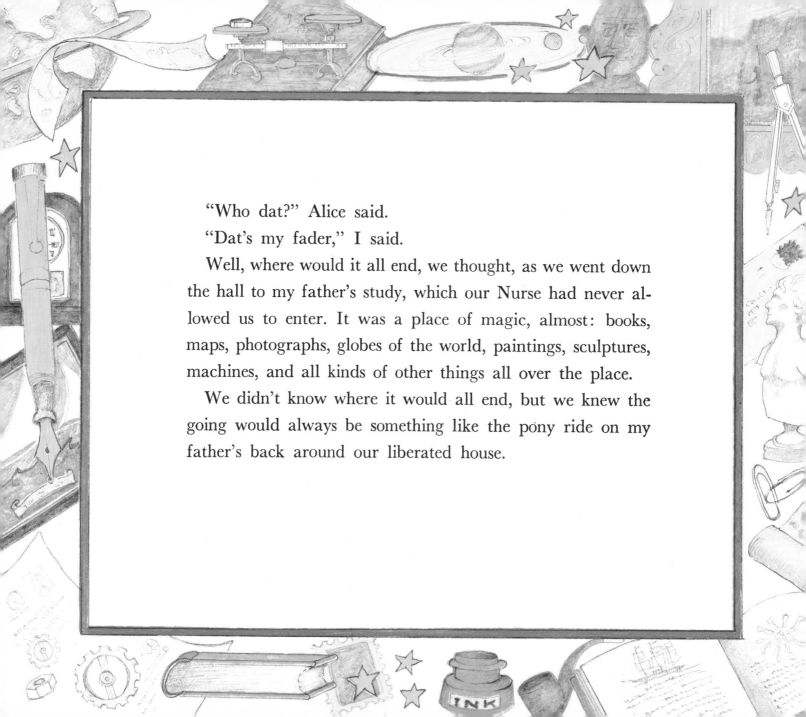

"Who dat?" Alice said.

"Dat's my fader," I said.

Well, where would it all end, we thought, as we went down the hall to my father's study, which our Nurse had never allowed us to enter. It was a place of magic, almost: books, maps, photographs, globes of the world, paintings, sculptures, machines, and all kinds of other things all over the place.

We didn't know where it would all end, but we knew the going would always be something like the pony ride on my father's back around our liberated house.